This book is dedicated to
Joel, Ramona & Arlo

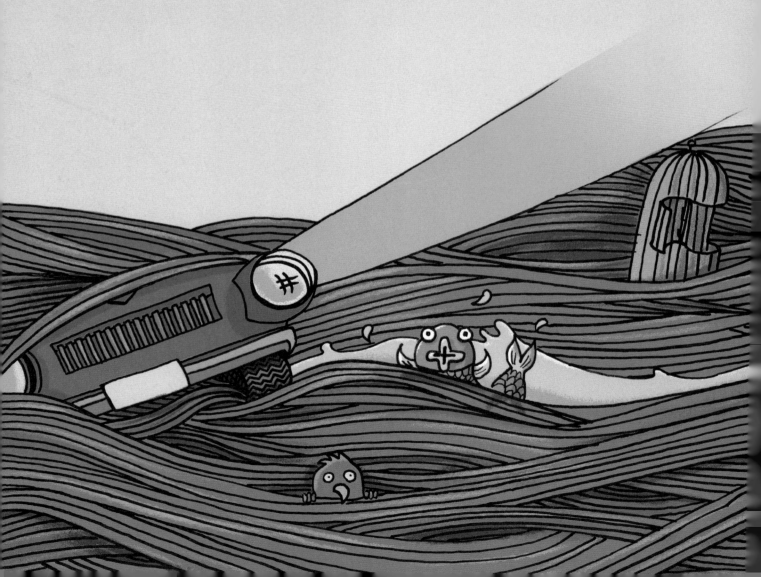

THE WORLD IN ROGER'S BEARD

Written by Anna Sweet

Illustrated by Robbie Graham

Roger's beard was deep and wide and mighty.
It was the biggest, bushiest beard anyone had ever seen!

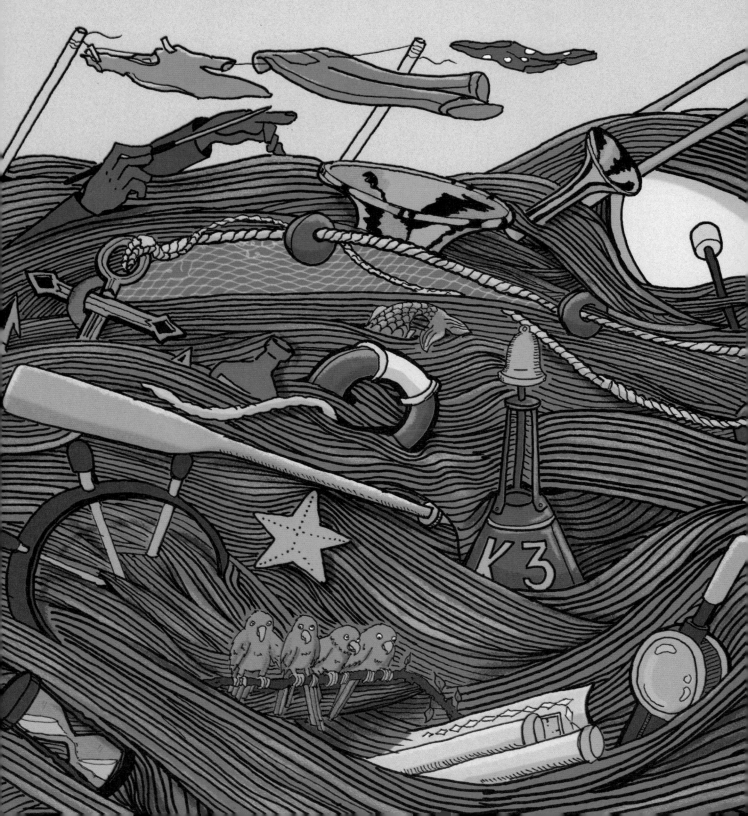

On the wispier whiskery bits some crusty old flakes of sea salt had dried many years ago, back when Roger was still sailing the seven seas.

Now, he simply uses it to season his chips.

It was always lovely and warm in Roger's beard and on cold and stormy nights all sorts of creatures came from far and wide to take shelter within his whiskers. Roger didn't mind, it was always nice to have company.

He liked to take tea with the turtle,

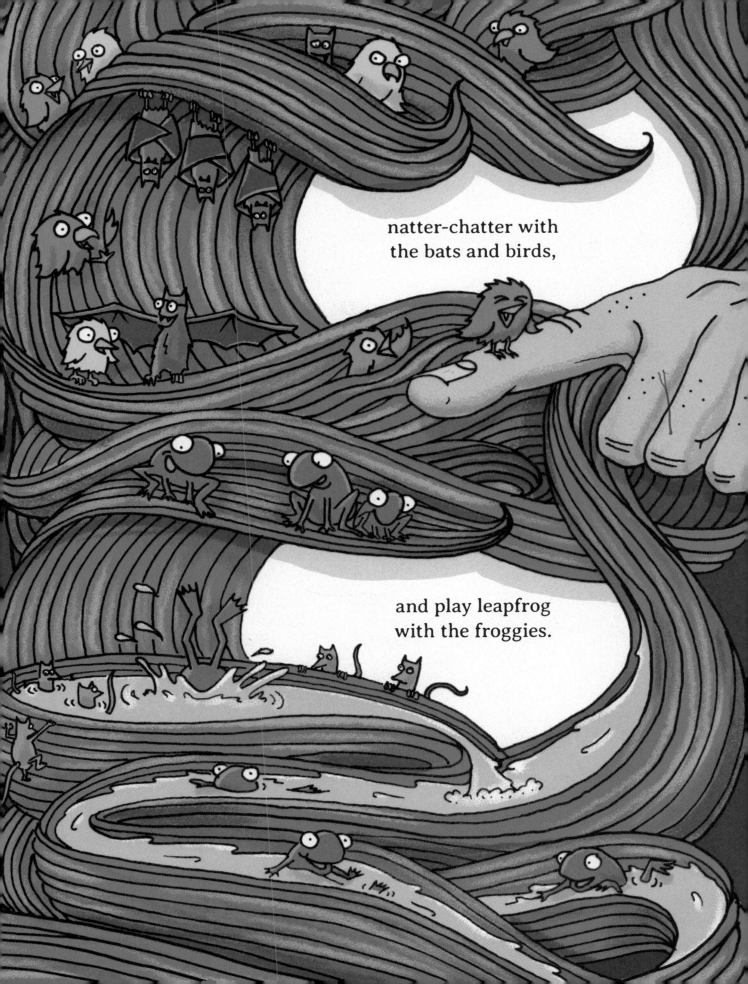

But sometimes, when Roger was out and about, strange and unusual NOISES could be heard coming from the beard...

And strange SMELLS too.

With all the wonders that lived inside, it made such
a hullabaloo that sometimes, Roger wished for peace and quiet.
He wished the turtles would talk amongst themselves,
he wished the froggies would stop hopping and bopping
and he wished the birds would just close their beaks for five minutes!

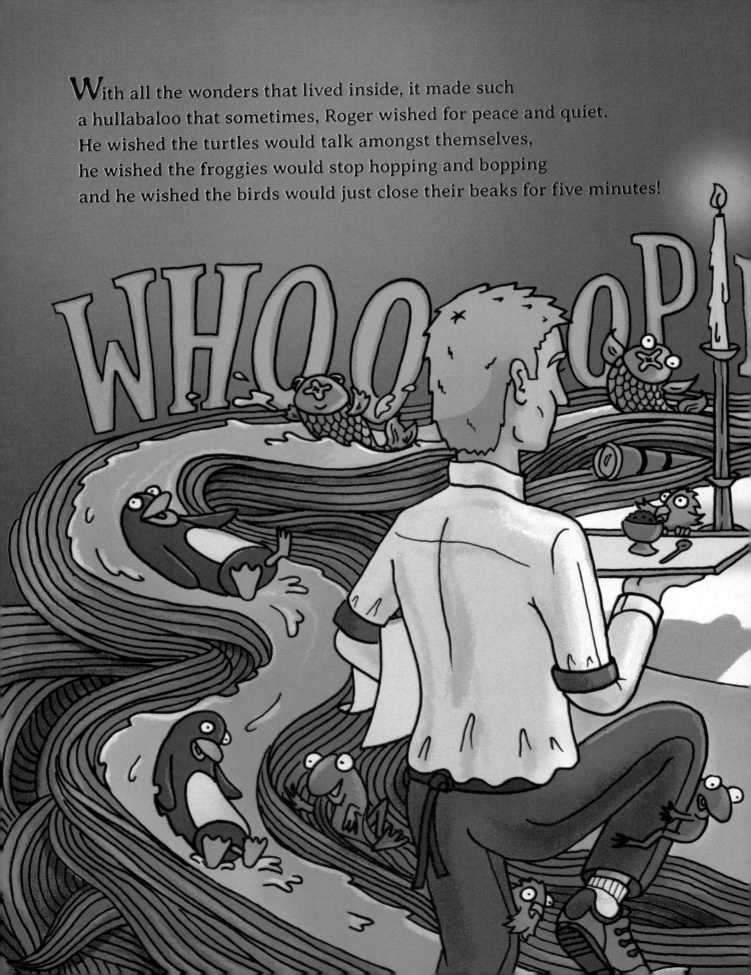

One day, Roger decided enough was enough.
"THAT'S IT..."

One by one, they flapped and flew, trundled and scuttled, leapt and wandered away, leaving Roger's beard empty for the first time in as long as he could remember.

Later that night he lay in his bed, listening to
the tick tock of the clock and the twit-twoo of the owls.

"It's very quiet,"

whispered Roger to himself, in his empty room.

With just the sound of birdsong in the trees and the smell of the wind for company, Roger thought of his friends. He remembered taking tea with the turtle, chattering and nattering with the birds, playing leapfrog with the froggies and he felt a feeling he had never felt before.

"I must find my friends!"

said Roger.

So he looked high,

he looked over,

he looked inside,

One by one, he found all of the froggies, rescued every bat and collected every bird. And when everyone was safely nestled back in his beard, he put the kettle on to make tea for all of his old friends...

and quite a few new ones too.

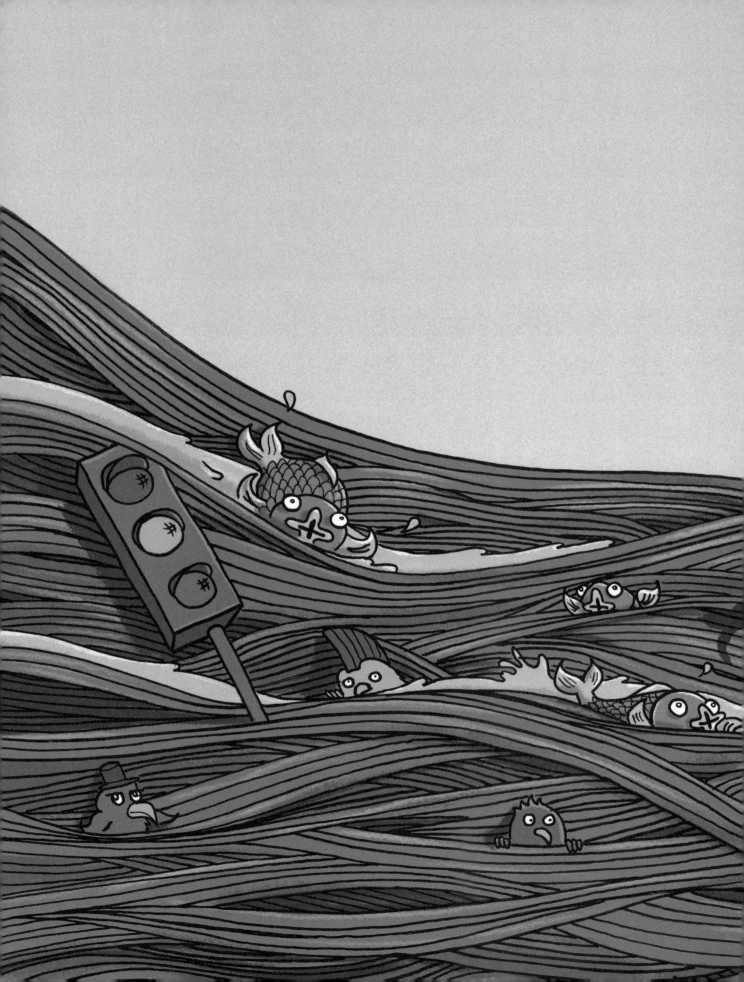

Printed in Great Britain
by Amazon